A Stop at the Lake

CATHERINE MALASKI • LISA PERRETT

Eve skips to the lake.

She can spin
and snap.

Eve stops.

She scans the lake for a swan.

HONK!

Eve spots a
red rose.

The rose smells nice.

SNIFF
SNIFF

Eve is stuck on
the stem.

ACK!

Swan, can you cut
the snag?

SNAP!
SNIP!

Thank you, Swan.

Swim home now.

scan(s)	sniff	stem
skip(s)	snip	stop(s)
smell(s)	spin	stuck
snag	spot(s)	swim
snap		

Decodable Words

ack	Eve	on
at	home	red
can	lake	rose
cut	nice	she

High-Frequency Words

a	is	the
and	now	to
for	swan	you
honk	thank	